BALLAD OF A GO

Title

OSHO OLAMILEKA

Author

foreverbabysincerely

Pen Name

TABLE OF CONTENT

ABOUT THE AUTHOR

God used my parents and they did the great work – foreverbabysincerely.

Osho Olamilekan Saheed, dandy of distinguished fame, born on June 30, 1996 in the small town of Mushin, Lagos Nigeria, hails from Ode Remo, Remo North Local Government, Ogun state. Osho Olamilekan is a skilled shoemaker, having learned the Art and Craft from two separate masters in 2012 and 2013 respectively, as he grew amidst two (2) siblings, all boys, Lekan is the middle child.

Olamilekan attended Temitope Nursery and Primary School, Shomolu, and in 2006, he proceeded in furtherance of his secondary education to CMS Grammar School, Akoka; the first secondary school in West Africa, all white, all boys school of Anglican foundation. In 2007, Olamilekan conceived the idea to start writing music. In partnership and Friendship with Ike Jeremiah and Bolu Adekanye, they created a Boy Band they called, **LIL BRIGGS**. Even though he was a Commerce Major, Olamilekan fell in love with Literature under the principal, Ven. Tunde Oduwole, he also learned polished etiquette and chivalry, he was Class Captain for several seasons of his 6year education duration, President of the Press club, President of the Literary and debating society and in his graduating year he was awarded Social Prefect on account of his ability to manage and control a team to achieving specific objectives, he represented the school in several victorious events, from poetry, to dance and drama. It is funny to say but Olamilekan's first role model is Fela Anikulapo Kuti, whence he learned artistic eccentricity. It was in 2012 while he completed his secondary education that he was baptized by the Arch Bishop of the Lagos Diocese.

After obtaining his O'level certificate, Olamilekan learned Shoemaking and leather work along with two childhood friends; Babajide Odunsi & Bosun Adebajo, under the supervision of His Excellency, Bagstowe, the Local Government Chairman of the Local Council at the time. The first time Olamilekan went into the shoemaker's shop, he made a wallet by the close of the day. Then he perfected leathery under the tutorship of his first cousin, Olusegun Sogbetun, a master of the Art. Afterwards, he created his own brand name; **HUSH CORDWAINER.**

In January 2013, Olamilekan completed his Admission registration in the Federal University of Agriculture Abeokuta, where he chose to study Entrepreneurship. Olamilekan is outstanding, always have been, on account of his cumulative grade point, he graduated with a Second Class Upper. During the time, he was known for Fashion and Modeling. Olamilekan is the first model to make appearance in the university Photo bucket. In 2016, Olamilekan made exclusive appearance in VOGUE Italia, having modeled for Bloke, Faith Oluwajimi, alongside, Osho Babajide his elder brother, a remarkable photographer in Nigeria and Tobiloba Oke, a close friend and Model.

It was in 2017, Olamilekan fell in love, well, that he says in all his stories. He published his first manuscript on Wordpress in 2018, titled **Parrot Carrot Tarot Judas Iscariot**. He realized he could actually chase the writer's dreams, and with fantastic plots and ideas over the years, he has since published up to 20 stories in the cloud.

September 2018, Olamilekan was drafted in the National Youth Service Corp and was deployed to Nasarrawa state, in the Northern Region of Nigeria, and in 2019, he was called up by MILES International in Lagos, under the ownership of Dr. Umoh Aniette, and supervision of Adeyanju Tobi; his cousin, to coordinate and execute strategies in the marketing department of Magnificent Cinemas. Olamilekan enrolled in the Education section of Community developmental service, and was liable to teach children in secondary schools in Eti Osa Local Government, Lagos, he taught Literature in English. He was awarded a Project Management Professional Certificate and a Certificate of Supply Chain and Logistics by the Project and Safety Management Institute.

After successfully completing the National Youth Service, Olamilekan bought a Kodak Camcorder from the hands of a friend and started to document 'everyday life' in Lagos. He made video skits for several actors and low budget music videos for upcoming artists in Nigeria, and the United State. Before the COVID 19 outbreak in 2019, Olamilekan gained admission to study Masters of Science in Management in the University of Lagos (UNILAG). In 2021, studying Masters in Management, Olamilekan ventured in the music business, he has since been managing several artists such as NARLTI, Skongz and a few others. In 2024, Olamilekan graduated from the University of Lagos with a Master's of Science in Management, having defended his Research project on 'Government policies and Entrepreneurial development in Nigeria' in May 2023. He was awarded a Certificate of Publishing by Notion Press in India, after successfully publishing Ballad of a golden girl.

Characters:

- Arnold, the Subjugator : The Supreme Emperor
- Courtroom Deputy : Old lady in court
- Ólafur : Protagonist
- Ingrid : Ólaf's mother
- Dmitri : Ólaf's father
- Roman J. Esq. : Ólaf's foster parent
- Lord Velvet : Noble Lord
- Apostle : Antagonist
- Desdemona : Daughter of Apostle
- Bishop : Son of Apostle
- Agatha: Wife of Apostle, Mother of Desdemona and Bishop.
- Heinrich : Dancer, Bologna brother
- Cicero : Singer, Bologna brother
- Margaret: A woman
- Duchess Adara: Wife of Lord Campbell II
- Abigail : The Waitress
- Francois : Another broken Soldier
- The button-man : Assassin
- Consuela : Haitian old lady
- Prince Charming Sej: Sejius, son of Narcissus (half brother of Arnold).
- Chevalier : The Rat
- Esteban : Thug
- Lord Campbell II : Noble Lord
- Isadora : Wife of Roman J. Esq.
- Penelope : Second wife of Roman J. Esq.
- Glover J. Esq. : Roman J. Esq.'s Grandfather

- Lady & Duchess in the audience: Voices in the courtroom.
- Nersus : Unknown Enemy

Each character names further paints a clearer picture of physical features attributed to them, because of their descent and origin. It is one beautiful unification.

Themes: Love, Crime, Friendship & Loyalty, Heroism, Eroticism, Money, Power.

Setting: From the 1940s throughout the 1950s to the 60s, in a contemporary world forged from the mind of the author where no man is subject to race, country or color. Each character is described as they are to create a clear picture of scenery. It is a made up world riddled in the ruins of war, with the people divided into; the powerful and the poor. It is a dirty world but the characters bring color.

Mary Boulevard: A made up country

Autumn Cello: The only press in Mary Boulevard, owned by Roman J. Esq.

Unicorn Ln: A street in Mary Boulevard

Cornflower fields: The War zone

Ko Tao: An island in the gulf of Thailand

Apostle's Triangle: A Citadel, owned by Apostle.

NOTABLE DATES

1963: Present day.

1930: Birth date.

1945: Ólaf was 15yrs old.

1947: Desdemona was 15yrs old when she first met Ólaf, he was 17.

1950: Desdemona was 18yrs and in love.

1956: During the war on CornFlower Fields.

1957: Ólaf is 27yrs and the war is over, and then comes Duchess Adara.

1960: Face-Off

PROLOGUE

Lord, don't forsake me.

What is this puppy love? –

'foreverbabysincerely, you are needed by everybody as a matter of global urgency'. I pushed my word count from a novelette to a novella, indeed ballad of a golden girl would take me to Hollywood, in search of a great perhaps, it was looking for Alaska that changed my entire life.

When money and power compete, everyone is silent, I took my time and pain to learn contentment, but these privileged individuals cannot get over jealousy. The spirit is the most important dueling in the universe, it is therefore important to walk/work with the spirit, the Holy Spirit.

I wrote a book that would bring the average man to tears. I cried on my paper, I cried to the screen, my tear dropped on this script, I put a lot of work into it, I am overwhelmed by my talent. Most importantly, I appreciate you all (my contacts), my ghost readers, I don't know who you are, but thank you. I wrote the most crucial plots on this green screen.

Ballad of a golden girl; what I love most is the cover design. It took a lot to arrive at the book title; I just wanted to write something Golden about a Girl. A Golden Girl, my mind is golden, so I put it to use. I painted picture perfect with the most beautiful words in the glossary, its going. Then I told the truth, I explained what happened in our little organization, ballad of a golden girl, I cried many times.

Yeah, we did it together, nobody is happier about this book than I am. The fact that I wrote it; Hadley Chase, Bernard Shaw, Hemingway, Fitzgerald with the magic touch of Vincent Van Gogh, Michelangelo and Dante Alighieri. I came to the conclusion, I wanted it to be a Ballad, a love poem, make everyone cry. I created a perfect character for my protagonist; his name is Ólafur, Ólaf for short. Tall, dark, handsome in a rugged way; a textbook lover. He can be best described with words, deep voice like a story teller; he wears pink oxford suits and Espadrille. He went to war on Cornflower field and returned a celebrity. I would not say how he acquired his wealth, so keep reading the book.

Chapter One

Sweet poet of a baby

{JUNE 6, 1963, Present Day}

In the giant court room stood a sign 'men cry, soldiers don't'. It was more like a brainwash to bottle up the hardship and pain intrinsic. The majestic throne was a statue of Arnold himself dressed in a warrior's armor. His chair is affixed to the face of the humongous statue, so his voice echoed from above, around the room with deep high pitch, everyone heard him clearly. Arnold invented superiority and made god of himself. The courtroom is occupied by three hundred Lords and Lady, two hundred Ecclesiastes, with five thousand denizens.

Courtroom deputy: (a white old lady with wrinkled face and hands, squinting in her thick lens spectacles like she was partially blind; she'd look up and down at the typewriter on her desk then steal another look at the audience, and then back at her typewriter, she was attentive like an Owl). Let the witness come in and take a bow.

Chevalier, the Rat, a short, dark, chubby man with a scar across his left eye, who seemed to sweat a lot walks in with a text book in hand, he takes a bow.

Courtroom deputy: you may speak Monsieur Chevalier.

Chevalier: you did not offer me a seat (the audience giggles).

Courtroom deputy: (assessing Chevalier from her spectacles) Sit, Monsieur Chevalier.

Chevalier locked himself in the leather arm chair at the center of the courtroom, cleared his throat and took a sip of water from the cup on the glass table.

Courtroom Deputy: you may speak Monsieur Chevalier.

Chevalier: Great Emperor, my name is Chev… Chevalier, I have come to tender reports on the triple murder at the Triangle with concrete evidence pertaining to Roman J. Esq. murder mystery. You see, I am a… I am (breaks down in tears).

ARNOLD: (audibly) don't cry soldier.

Chevalier's eyes glowed, tears disappear, it was an honor to be in the presence of the Great Arnold, the subjugator. He swallowed saliva and continued his speech.

Chevalier: I met a great mind on Cornflower fields: he was a simple writer and a bouncing lover, only his smile would light up this courtroom. The only single man I met who has hope. He gave me a book, I will read from his account, the book.

Courtroom Deputy: do as you please Monsieur Chevalier, just don't cry.

Chevalier adjusts his tie and begins to read.

{Flashback}

Ólafur spoke less, only to the waitress and lieutenant colonel. He was tall, handsome in a rugged way, with tiny eyes and a vampire smile affixed to his face, his deep voice like a story teller, more often than not, his emotions rose to a crescendo when he was alone, he would soliloquy and cry. Born on June 30, 1930, he grew upon the farm outside Mary Boulevard, with his mother, Ingrid, she was a poetess. Ólafur was born of true love in the struggling times. Dmitri, his father, was a Goldsmith, he was gun down the rapid fire the day Ólafur was born, neither did he see his son nor was he given a proper burial. Ingrid named her son Ólafur not only to commemorate his father but she thought it had some poetry to it. Ólaf for short, which he preferred, reminded Ingrid of the men she loved, whom she had lost; his father, her father. Like Dmitri, Ólafur was artist, he too was obsessed with orderliness, and his mother loved that about him. When he was 6yrs old, he spent alone time in the open fields, writing poetry about sunset and dawn, he wrote songs about Birds and Ladybug, he fantasizing about girls, he had no formal education, and Ingrid did the tutoring.

August 6, 1945

He was 15 when Ingrid died of Pneumonia, Ólaf lived in the Orphanage homes, which he hated a lot, it was there and then he met Roman J Esq. -J for Jeremiah. He owned the only Press on Mary Boulevard called 'Autumn Cello'. All he saw was Ólaf's handwriting and he took a liking to him. Ólaf joined the Autumn Cello and published manuscripts for the local magazine, 'the orphan secretary-hand' Roman J. Esq. would call him. Roman J. Esq. brought Ólaf into his home where he lived alone, and he taught him the Oxford way, Ólaf published up to 500 manuscripts through the years, Roman J Esq. taking all the credits. That was his way of taking back from Ólaf; after all there isn't any free lunch. Roman J. Esq. did not have a humble beginning, he was born with silver spoon, his Grandfather Glover J Esq. owned plenty art. His timeless wealth is reflected in his generation. Roman J Esq. met his first wife, Isadora, in law school; she bore him 2 female children and lost to cancer at 35. Then Roman J Esq. met his second wife, Penelope, 3 years after Isadora's death. Sadly, she was barren, Roman J Esq. wanted a male child desperately, but he stopped trying when the doctors informed him of his *Myotonic Dystrophy*. He did not take the news in over his head however, he lived his normal life. Then he met Ólaf at the orphanage and took him home. He was a tall, handsome man; he looked like a blend of Mediterranean and African with Middle Eastern influences. He always wore Flap Pockets no matter the occasion and he kept an imperial mustache. His cologne was strong as the scent of a corpse, everyone knew he was around, he chokes everyone and they were used to it. He was always full of delight and never lost his temper.

One beautiful faithful Thursday evening, August 12, 1947, there was feelings; the Noble Lord and Ecclesiastics graced the office of Roman J. Esq. for the publication of a manifesto. In person of Lord Velvet and Apostle.

Roman J. Esq.: Good day Noble Lords, to what may I grace this August visit, my esteemed? I have wine and bread, most of all; I have the most beautiful secretary hand with the finest glossary to draft the most enthralling manifesto in the history of paper- ink.

Indeed, Roman J. Esq. may be artistic but he was a brilliant negotiator. The Lord Velvet and Apostle stayed 12 hours longer in Autumn Cello and at the 13th, the doors were finally open. The escorts arrived in Caravans, the manifesto was conveyed with utmost care, Ólaf followed behind Roman J. Esq. as the Lord Velvet and Apostle led. Two guards open the caravan doors and the innocent flowery daughter of Apostle jumps out and run to the embrace of her father; The first time Ólafur set his eyes on Desdemona, he knew everything would change, alas his wretched life would have a meaning, immediately, his life flashed before his eyes in a split second with the speed of light, he saw a life long struggle to have a girl as innocent and pure as she was. Thoughts of his childhood in the farm, the embrace of his mother, his new father, he was not entitled to any of The J Esq. wealth, or even Roman's from whom he learned the life of fine etiquette. She was Tangerine in color, her eyes were green and her cheeks were blushing red. She wore Coral Frocks and ballerina shoes with green bracelets that matched with the color of her eyes. Her teeth were milky and she used braces. She was 15 and Ólaf fell in love right away.

Two years after the inauguration, Feb 14, 1949, a grand feast was held in Apostle's triangle. The triangle was not only the oldest castle in Mary Boulevard; history had it that the first suicide was committed in the Triangle. It is also rumored that people had gone missing within its walls, in truth, it was Desdemona's Rapunzel castle and she had let her hair down. Ólaf had been sneaking into her ward for over 13 months, they were in love, blooming teenagers.

The room was slightly illuminated by the moon shaped standing lamp on the dresser; the thick purple curtains were wide open so the room is properly ventilated. The room stench like sweat, tears and passion with a mix of romance and hot wild sex, Desdemona's tangerine skin cements upon Olaf's brown body and they made colorful mixture on the bed which is assumed to be the palette. Desdemona moans softly, her voice lowered in his ears like she was trying to whisper something, but she was too consumed by orgasm and she continues to moan, gently. Ólaf stretched out her body horizontally on the bed frame, sweat drop roll down his broad chest, her feet arched with artistry, he bites on her toe, the red nail polish tasted like berry on his lips. She was creamy so every thrust of his tool made a sloppy noise, and a wet slap. He was rock hard in her cabbage. As he reached climax, he groan and spew poetry, like…

Ólaf: I've been falling from the moon, and I need a safe landing, I'm grabbing onto the hips of Mama Saturn. Desperate me, holding on to grace for dear life, pondering the wonders of the stars and how they merge with her dark green eyes. Her skin illuminate with artistic pleasure, like early morning sun ray, bewildering my heart, making mockery of my intelligence because I am stupid in her presence. My apple tree; if your lip would save me, let your kiss be my dying wish.

Desdemona: oh sweet boy, what have you done, you are wild, you roam free in my mind.

Ólaf: You look in the eyes of a man... broken man, as a form of redemption. Your smile is hypnotic and your aura is enchanting. You believe so many things, oh yet I question everything. You play your love like the squid game; men will die in your name; red light, green light, all the women light up the world, yet I only catch your color.

Ólaf rolls Desdemona over, her back arched over on her two knees, like a cat, Ólaf gently scratch her skin up from her thigh, making a snarling noise as he bite softly on her buttock, like a wild animal, Desdemona heave a deep sigh, Ólaf spanks her arse and she wailed with eroticism.

Desdemona: oh dearest sweet boy, you words are like magic, but you're not born of noble blood, papa will have your head, then I'd die too, oh sweet boy, love make you a wicked boy!

Ólaf: I am only a victim of love at first sight, I bless the heavens that you're alive, but without you, I'm dead.

He ejaculates hot semen in her ovary; they lay on the bed shamelessly as Desdemona sobs on Ólaf's chest.

■■

{FAST FORWARD; THE WAR}

September 13, 1956, Ólaf had not made peace with his heart broken to pieces. Some days, he'd lay on the bed in a dark shade, crying. The Comrades would walk in, they knew he loved the girl *like bastard.* The Generals summoned for a war correspondent to document battle details concerning the opponent's heavy artillery and sophisticated technology. Ólaf was drafted by the men in power in 1952, he already knew Apostle was trying to get rid of him, sending him to the front line to die, he could have gone on exile but he obliged. He wanted to prove to Desdemona that he could fight for her love, he was willing to die for her love. His flesh had grazed the battle grass for four years, he had watched his comrades burn and die in the brutal siege. The Generals had a name for it, Cornflower fields. Ólaf had managed to survive, and he delivered exceptional services in the frontline by documenting reports on Nersus's powerful military operation, aiding ARNOLD's army in tactical strategy formation leading to victory. He wrote more poems and ballad, he tried to complete his big story. He wrote in his textbook;

"I am coming or maybe I'm too late, some of us learn poetry from dialogues in movies, some of us touch ourselves to sleep. It's just good, it feels good to have someone beside, someone you can take care of and look after, someone you can bear with, someone you can cohabit with, someone who knows your excesses, someone who is hopeful about your adventures, someone who can ride with you, or guide you, someone who understands you, that you Jonze. Someone; the missing ribs of your bone. Tears of calypso, as I set sail in the setting sun, she calls me from a séance, I burn sage in her remembrance."

19 October, 1957

Perfect evening In Unicorn Ln; Orange sky, setting sun, the streets was buzzing with people running home to their tattered shelter; the blind banker and her aide, the boys and girls had just taken their bath, the prostitutes were underage, the street was littered with portholes and water filled them to the brim, residents had gotten used to it, and the air was anosmic, odorless but a little comforting. Ólaf walked into the third building on the right before the gate at the entrance, it was his favorite pub.

The waitress always listens, Abigail, she is accustomed to broken men, she's seen variety. Every now and then, broken men are in her presence, she has few things to say; pour more, want more, another round, men do the talking.

Abigail: ready to order?

Ólafur: I'll have the Triple Berry… and the Steak please… with St Morris.

The liquor sinks deeper with cigarettes, he continued writing; *"I found love, love left me –still in love…"* then he stopped. His eyes travelled around the Pub in his round cut dark shade spectacle. Underneath the pink oxford suit and Espadrille, he had seen the outcome of war, seven years of blood spill, now promoted but not noble, he was only a celebrity. He did all the fighting on Cornflower fields for the love of a lady who was once a child, now she's grown. He preferred the empty Pub, he thought and shrugged, he had walked in one day and someone else had taken his favorite seat, another soldier in the abyss. He settled in another seat and took time to listen to the soldier's story. He had just returned from Cornflower fields, his uniform concealed the battle scars, scars that were mirrored in his gaze, a man who went by the name Francois.

Abigail: Pour more?

Ólaf: yes, refill please.

Ólaf told the waitress to fill him up; Francois did not look up.

Francois: fill my cup!

Then he began to talk about the camp and battlefields, he talked about few soldiers against heavy artillery. He talked about reinforcement; he dropped his head in disappointment. He talked about his fellow soldiers, then he looked at Ólaf, "……have you carried your brother's pain, shouldered his burden, and carried him across sea, protecting his lifeless body against mercenaries….. ALL FOR NOTHING" (banging his wrapped fist on the table). Francois wanted to say more, but Olaf was not his priority, he paid for more beer and Abigail paid attention. The woman in the counter; he wanted her to listen to what he had coming.

Francois: Margaret, Margaret … Margaret, I started finding joy. Margie like her mother calls, she let me down. She was a street urchin before she met me, I made her feel blessed, I was poor but I bought her silver jewelries, because they fit her better in silk dress. She said she'd change her ways. She made a vow in the rain before Cornflower field, it was simple; she'd wait. She thought I would die or disappear, so she sorts the other soldiers for company while I was gone. She is still unmarried but with a son, pour me another drink (Abigail fills François' cup). She couldn't look me in the face, let alone speak. Margaret is a toxic woman; she too had poison like the viper. She believes she can make any man succumb with a swing of her hips, but she did not have many good things to say because of her troubled past. That is why she prey on men, she believes a woman's power lies in the voice of a powerful man, so she must possess the loudest, most powerful if not she could even hurt herself. She preys on the conscience of innocent men, they always want to be better for her, I thought I was tough, I am mesmerized how she mess my mind.

From time to time Francois would gnash his teeth, he was suffering from PTSD, alcohol tragedy but the loss of his dear Margaret was rapidly killing him.

Francois: "I should not be saying this, but you remind me of Margaret, you have the same lustrous eyes, you look like Margaret, all women look like Margaret."

Then he looked at Ólaf, eye balls deep and asked if he had cigarette. Ólaf responded that he had 2 left.

'You have hope', Francois said and left. Ólaf looked down at his textbook and realized he had written more words in his big story.

"We had just met, and I was with another girl, she moved with me to the new house, she wanted to live closer to me, she wanted to see me every day and supervise everything I was doing, so she moved in and she charmed me. She's tall; complete body feature, she's bright, she paints, she draw. I write and I'd never met a girl so artistic. These were the things she did to get me. I left my girl for her love- 3 Weeks later; I told her I could not do it anymore. Lucky for her she found someone she could love. I sacrificed that love for my Golden Girl. My Golden Girl had no one, but she seemed like she'd been broken before. The first time we fucc was the first time I fucc'd, she had been fucc'd before. I did not ask who fucc'd her, she did not want to talk of her past, I wanted to keep fucc'n her, I was concerned about my future. We fucc'd a lot. We fucc'd on the bed and on the floor, on the table and on the fridge, the bathroom and kitchen floor. We

fucc'd outside, we fucc'd on her period, we fucc'd raw. Her blood was my communion; I guess I'm fucc'd for life. She locked me in a dark room for the next few months, I did not eat her food, but I ate watermelon. She was watery, always watery, so I knew she was a goddess, she squirts… I was lucky. The other girls wanted to live like her, they were jealous of what I had, she made me proud. Some will tell me they love how she dresses, some will say she's gentle, some loved her, my friend was in love with her and I was possessive. Art was the base of our love, and we were stringed by the heart for love, it was much fun when we made love."

The war was finally over, he would not be seeing Abigail any longer and after 7 years, all she deserved was the tip. He walked out of the pub and took a deep breath, it smelled like October, his conscious mind had always prepared him for incoming troubles, but it was the little old Haitian lady, Consuela who welcomed him with a smile then handed him a flower, Amaryllis, that distracted him; for the first time that Summer, Ólaf smiled, but only for a moment.

Ólaf: when would you stop with the flowers, Consuela?

Consuela: when you tell me what you fear the most my dearest sweet man.

'Maybe today would be different', he thought.

He had been holding back tears, his emotions became expressionless and he wanted to feel something.

'Tonight, I would cry', he concludes.

It was then it made obvious, the black Sedan parked on the street since he arrived. He shoved the flower into his trench coat carefully and adjusted this dark shade spectacle, and then he walked on. The night before, anxiety had taken the best of him; he had little sleep drowning himself in Whiskey, watching monochrome slideshow of bitter memories. He had to take medications because of the ache in his ankle; it was the whiskey that kept him stable. The tumor in his brain, nights like this he wishes it would explode, the pills were not helping, he cursed the nurse for not prescribing Morphine, instead she went on and on talking about good music as a therapy, healing mechanism, or whatever she said…

'I am disappointed in myself, now and then I flip the pages of the past, I am haunted by shadows of make believe. I fall back to addiction; I'm alone now more than ever. All I have to beseech is the poetry in this script, maybe this would make me a better being. The addictions serenade my sorrow, I am hooked on expensive drug, save me.'- he thought loud -*I do not fear Nersus, I do not fear Apostle, I fear Women. I remember the Bologna Brothers, I also think about them when I am alone.*

It was terrible, the outcome of the war, for me the greatest loss were the brothers –Heinrich the dancer, Cicero the singer / they complemented one another. They looked alike; they enjoyed being called brothers even though they were only friends. With tremendous outcome in the first 4 years of the great siege, they were noticed by everyone, their bond was strong like a knot fastened for mountain climbing. It was a special bond they shared in every straight sense of it. One remarkable event, the brothers led an ambush with agility, they forced the Nersus army to retreat, and the brothers were exalted. It was the moment due for promotion that the woman came, the woman who would tear their brotherhood apart. If Heinrich had known better he would have left the woman and let the Cicero love her. He said too much, he did too much. He knew better when he lost everything; his brother, the friendship, it felt like a competition with him. She whispered jealousy and envy into Heinrich's ears then she gave love to the Cicero, so they saw nothing but hate in one another. Cicero would kill to impress the woman and Heinrich's constant reminder of Cicero's vulnerability steered enmity, then she became a bridge to their friendship, their brotherhood, till she collapsed right between them. There are two sides to the story, I was watching, so ask me.

The bullet grazed us on Cornflower field, our lives flashed before our eyes. Heinrich looked up at Cicero, who had now lost faith in their friendship, - are you going to watch me, sinking? Heinrich cried. Cicero's eyes pierced deep into Heinrich's, feeling nothing. He once believed in him, they were more like brothers, they'd fought, danced and cried side by side in the war against Nersus, till a woman came between them, only a woman could. The brothers had it planned out, mapped out, they were destined for victory so long as they had one another, but a woman came, oh a woman, bless a woman, curse a woman, she remains a woman, she came and she set fire to the tree of friendship, she was only doing her thing.

Heinrich: I don't know what she told you in the dark room but you have to believe me because I'm your brother, not once have I misled you. For old time sake, my friend.

Cicero picked up a hand gun and cocked it, taking aim at Heinrich; he closed one eye and balanced the other on his focus.

Cicero: you've always been the famous one, I tagged along, you fed off people's attention, I was just another decoration. I do not need any approval from you to love who ever I chose, and if I cannot love her, then I can only hate you.

Heinrich: I thought I was helping you (he cries).

Cicero: (he smirks) I was using you.

His eyes colored red with blood veins full of rage launched the bullet into Heinrich's skull and his brain splattered. But things would look better for Olaf, he'd make it out of the mud, although he had no one, he'd frequent the pub. The sound of liquor pour in cup was music to his ears, and every gulp, his sorrow seemed disappear. Come to think of it, Margaret her name was.

Chapter Two

Roman J Esq. a murder mystery

{FLASHBACK; JULY 2, 1950}

A family dinner in Apostle's Triangle, the elite dine like Chinese, different dish on the table. There was sparkling water in separate Jugs, distinguished by their flowery designs. Lazy Susan, Pancake, Pastries, Eggs and Butter on a Caramel tray. Fried Rice, Jollof and coconut rice with Salad on a round Walnut tray. Lobsters, Barracuda, Shrimps and Cod in separate Tupperware. Chicken Masala, Peruvian style roast Chicken with Green sauce, Onions and dental floss spread across with serviettes, silver spoons, and gold plates. Fruits; Apples, Oranges , Bing Cherries, Montmorency Cherries, Blackberries, Strawberries, Cucumber and Veggies in the Centre of the round Bonsai Dining Table manufactured by Boca do Lobo, himself. Bishop recites the Lord's Prayer; Our father in heaven, as the scented Cedar-wood candles cleansed the air, while the Bergamot gave the calming scent.

Apostle, Desdemona, Agatha and Bishop sitting clock wise, bow their heads in prayer, such that Apostle and Agatha are seated opposite one another.

Bishop: Our father who Art in heaven, hallowed be thy name, thy kingdom come, thy will be done as it is in heaven. You give us today, our daily bread and forgive our trespasses as we forgive those who have trespassed against us, and lead us not into temptation, but deliver us from all evil.

Apostle: Amen.

Agatha and Desdemona: (in unison) Amen.

(Agatha looks at Desdemona and smile on one cheek, not very genuine).

Bishop: Amen (reaching for the pancake in a haste, Agatha passes the salad to Apostle and Desdemona bites apple).

Desdemona: papa, I have something important to discuss.

Apostle: (bites salad and drinks water, then raise his brows to look at his daughter) My apple, you know better than to speak at the dinner table.

Desdemona: papa, I had to wait till we're seated together as a family.

Agatha: (interrupt Desdemona calmly) you can at least wait till we have finished with our food.

Desdemona: (interrupts) it is about the new Tutor, Ólaf.

Apostle: (sharply, bangs a wrapped fist on the table) did anyone touch you inappropriately? (Bishop, who is shocked with a mouthful of Egg, froze on his seat as his eyes wandered about the other individual on the table).

Desdemona: (shamefully) No papa, I … I … I am in love with him.

Agatha: (vexed) be quiet child, what do you know of love, you are only Eighteen (a teen, 18).

Apostle eyes begins to glisten and water with fury; of all the noblemen in Mary Boulevard, Desdemona would rather settle for a peasant, a gaddemn orphan with mere polished literature. After all her studies and training in Princess Charm school. It was in that moment Apostle began to regret his actions- requesting Roman J Esq. brings his ward to teach his daughter shorthand. He sits quiet, short of words, almost sure he would strike Desdemona in the face, but he sits quiet.

Agatha: You don't know what you're saying child, don't be a fool.

Desdemona: Mother, I'm in love, what do you expect me to do? It's overwhelming.

Agatha: and what about Sej, he has grown in the ways of a charming prince.

Desdemona: Mother, you know Sej is no good, a dead beat. I am not interested in his money.

Agatha: keep quiet foolish child, if not for the money, you would not be born in this time.

Apostle gave a sharp look at Agatha, reminding her to be cautious of the things she said around the kids.

Apostle: Desdemona my apple, not only do you mock me, but you make jest of all I worked hard to achieve. Desdemona, my apple your choice of love is a dent to my name, and what I'm going to do next… (He whispers) is unspeakable.

Desdemona: (gets up from her seat angry, weeping) papa!! He's just a boy!!

Agatha: (snapping) sit and be quiet little child, is this what you learned in school?

Bishop: I should go to my room.

Desdemona: Sit there too Bishop, you're my brother.

Bishop: (remorseful, sits quietly cleaning his growing mustache with serviette).

Desdemona: (kneels before Apostle's feet) papa, I love him, there's nothing that can change that. Please I need you to understand.

At this point, Apostle knew his daughter's mind was made up. He stood and walked out of the dining room, Agatha hurried behind him. Apostle reached the door and halt, he did not turn but he said 'you must never speak his name under my roof', then he walks away.

Agatha: (reaches the door) look what you've done foolish child (chasing after Apostle).

■■

On the 4th day of September 1950, when Nersus struck, the first outbreak, Mary Boulevard was in disarray. Nersus had invented the Quinoa Explosive, more soldier were needed on Cornflower field. That morning on Mary

Boulevard, a parcel was sent to Autumn Cello, Chief Editor and Publisher in person of Roman J Esq. He was not expecting any package from the frontline but he figured it would be rude to ignore. He unwrapped the parcel and instantly, there was an explosion, Autumn Cello burned to the ground. Ólaf was twenty years old at the time, and once again orphaned.

Olaf moved to a bachelor sized condo in the old service apartment on Boulevard Ln, from where he first began writing his big story, he had not given any name to it, but he wanted to write something golden, about someone golden, with a golden pen and a golden mindset, for a golden girl. Desdemona was his muse; he knew if he published the story telling tales of forbidden love and torture, the world would be intrigued, he always thought that it would be his big break, so he put a lot into it.

Desdemona stomped into the room like she was mad about something. She was pacing around, he had learned from her temper, so till she cool off he did not make any sound. We cannot hide here much longer, she muttered. He was working on his big story; the publishers said they needed more. – Your rent is due, you cannot afford the condor, she continued. (Still silence) -My mother is worried Papa would do something, I'm leaving tomorrow. For a moment he'd stop typing on the typewriter, his eyes glued to the last words on the paper 'hers dangerously'. He knew the day would come, he envisaged her confrontation, even if she was hoarding some of the information; he already knew the full detail.

She walked to the gramophone and picked an old Afrobeats. She did no longer speak, as wise man would listen; listen deeply to the lyrics.

"Your mama say omo mi, no follow I never chop/ make you find correct guy/ no be love you go chop".

Indeed, she was admitting to his love, a love her family did not approve of, Ólaf thought silently. His thought could be bouncing all around the room and Desdemona would hear every bitty bit of it, but he remained calm and quiet, silence overwhelm. He dropped his head in disappointment, he knew she would say it eventually, he felt the muscles in his body shrink and his bones thicken, his phalanges dropped with force on the typewriter and his left ring finger clicked D. He kept staring at the letter, he tried to find meaning to it, something to take his mind off the sad energy radiating in his condo. She continued, 'I think you have a drinking problem'. 'I think she has a thinking problem', he thought. She thinks for everyone, he already told her to live and let nature take its course; but Desdemona; she's innocent, spoilt rich brat, she's selfish of course.

D for Desdemona; He was desperate, disgraced, yet deserving… Of all the words in the dictionary, he did not have a word to describe himself, maybe drunk again. But he deserved pity, he was a dreamer, maybe he was delusional but he deserved Desdemona. Damn, he couldn't live without her, they were departing… so he was good as dead. The love had done a number on him, he knew nothing else, and he loved her dangerously.

You don't speak, Desdemona charged, she's was not aggressive but she knew she was losing him. She knew better. Her father could not stand to hear the sound of his name. It rained fury and rage when Apostle barged into his condor the following morning; like he was not the type, he was not old money, trust fund baby, like he was not good enough for her. Even if Apostle knew he had the birds coming, he concluded that the orphan only wanted his daughter for her prowess.

She was not a happy person, more reserved, keeping things to herself, she only talks to Holy Mary, she hides her sorrow in a straight face, expressionless smiles, she would be forced to betroth Prince Charming. Apostle was cursed to carry to the weight of his daughter's heavy heart, so he sent Desdemona to a boarding school. He wanted her far away from the triangle, far away from the orphaned boy with beautiful calligraphy. Apostle wanted Ólaf gone. Apostle had mapped out a perfect life for his children; Desdemona and Bishop, he knew he had to fix them with the high rankings to retain his honor and grace in the eyes of ARNOLD. Bishop fought frontline with Prince Charming, Sej, he was gruesome, fearless, victorious, but Sej takes the glory. With Desdemona betrothed to Sej, she would be called her Majesty, or maybe Queen, and that was all Apostle wanted her to be.

Desdemona's first week in the boarding school for Princesses, she received a letter in the mailbox; it was stamped ~yours dangerously. Her heart melt, shrunk to liquid, hot tears roll down her eyes too salty. She couldn't believe she would live another day without Ólaf, she was not sure he would make it in the frontline, he was only a writer, even though he possessed a curious mind, he was still a gentle lover. But she had to move on, she had to focus on the things of the future, her father knew what's best for her, she thought. She would respond to Ólaf's letters in a notebook; a notebook she never sent out to him, it was her dark little secret.

'My Golden Girl always keeps a secret, once I was her secret. '

Ólaf ~ yours dangerously

I'm being too specific, because I cannot see you, I let my love travel overseas, my heart is sailing the Pacific. I'm trying to give you more than you would afford, my love is sufficient for the both of us. If it was up to me, I'd make your everyday like a holiday. Think about you? I do that every day. When I call and you mute like you don't know what to say, it bothers me to think anyone would take my place.

Desdemona ~ Textbook Lover

From fighting hard not to

To completely loving you

Each moment has been beautiful

Ólaf ~ yours dangerously

Many times I said I love you, another brother down... gliding into the abyss. You said we should work on our relationship, my heart dropped when the Army summoned me. If you ever got a sign from my eyes, you'd know it was my death sentence, all I have is the beautiful memories you left me. Fucc!

Desdemona ~ Textbook Lover

You say I love you

And I want to wrap my arms around you

Never let go

Tell you all my secrets

And bear out my soul

Ólaf ~ yours dangerously

The last time we came together to patch things up, we only made out in the Truck, leaving out the important things we had to discuss. I had fallen asleep when you snuck out and drove off. You are stretched out in my mind like a sacrifice on the altar, when I said "I love you", I did not stutter. I'm staring at our photographs and I remember; I remember in every pose and sound of the shutter. You're mine forever...

Desdemona ~ Textbook Lover

Sometimes I'm tired

Tired of everything

Tired of pretending

Tired of smiling

Tired of being empty

Then you show up

And I'm not so tired

Not in the cheesy dramatic way

But every time it's always enough

Ólaf ~ yours dangerously

We used to cuddle together... the Christmas we celebrated together. One day I'll tell my grandchildren the story of how I met their grandmother, but until they day, I'd be in love with you. When we were young, we would drive around in your Father's Ford, you would buy me Candy, Candy I could not afford. You were leaving for boarding school and I was scared of loosing you. Look how I lost you to the library and lecture room. I hope you remember who you are to me, because I do. I fill up the liquor in my cup and I begin to write about you because you are my muse. The dope no longer conjures you.

Desdemona ~ Textbook Lover

I should be reading but you've taken over all of my thoughts.

Desdemona went into depression, she was not a happy person, and she wanted Ólaf to be her joy. She did not have hope, she was his drug.

News of Ólafur's return from Cornflower fields carrying wealth and power reached Apostle. Just as he retreated to his grandiose bedroom to lay his head and sleep, Apostle blew out the candle by the corner of his bed; the fire went out leaving thick smoke in the room, choking slightly. Apostle understood the parable of the thick smoke, so he summoned a button man to eliminate Ólaf discretely, because he too had become a notable figure, important person, a celebrity in the war, following his award of Might and Valor; these things must be done neatly - Apostle commanded.

December 25, 1959

{7:27PM; THE WAR IS OVER}

Breezy evening in his Palazzo, Ólaf is captured alone, pacing around the balcony, his hands wrapped together behind on his buttock, his head dropped in disappointment. He finds his way to a wooden rocking chair in the balcony, adjusted his kimono, sitting slowly and calmly.

"I feel it very close, the green light in my grasp, I want to take it slow, but this breathe feels like my last. I want to cry, I'm crying, I am overwhelmed by my talent".

It is neither a dream nor a nightmare, where he could see her, only in silhouette. She eventually cut her hair. He was twenty when Desdemona left; now they were in their youth. *What do kids know?* They had both sprung from separate roots, she was old money and he did not make honest money. He thought if he had a little more going for himself, she would love him for his prowess, so he went to war and fought honorably, her wealth made shame of him, he would sit alone in the balcony of his Palazzo, with deep understanding of why she left him at the corridor, he traced his left thumb on his chest, and inserted it into the bullet hole between his breasts, only she had the access to penetrate, her thumb print is secure in his heart, she had touched him in many ways within a short space, in a small room where they had nobody to lean on but one another, they were in love every day, and every day was an understatement. They lived their life for loving each other; he did not want any other to carry his last name. Ólaf heaved a heavy sigh and adjusted the Cummerbund of his Aegean Kimono, he picked the ink and placed his textbook on the Honduran Mahogany table and flipped to the page he'd stopped writing then continued;

"She was upstairs with her friends and I was drunk that weekend, she was ashamed of me, yet I recite to her the best love poetry that exists under the sun. She did not believe in my talent anymore, she was too grown for that, she needed assurance. I respected her privacy but I wanted to be with her more, she does not walk with me on the street, we did that only once. I remember because it

happened only once. She loved me in the dark room where she was battling her demons, I comforted her soul, I listened to her breathe, her breath stink like stacks of money, but she is not so happy with everything, all the money and glamour, she's not like the regular spoilt little kids, jumping around in pearls and pajamas on Christmas eve, she gets her hands dirty with art and painting, she's a tremendous artist. She lives her life like art, so I study her. Then she makes me feel like a man, she never belittle me. Not till the day, she gave me sex like a corpse, I made love to a dead woman, and she looked into my eyes with a blank stare. It was terrifying, her soul had left me. Her love was my dress, I dressed in colors. I was shining, my happiness was contagious, and everyone around me could bare the testimony. She was happier with me, she was able to express herself, my love was white in her black dress, she became a polka dot, and she wouldn't admit that my love set her free. I wonder what her Mother thought when she first met me, beyond the good looks and lucky charm, she could see that I was slightly impoverished. I had nothing to offer but time and company -ooh lest I forget poetry. I did not have any money, her brother was disappointed, her father wouldn't even look her in the face, I was not enough, his message was clear. I do not blame my golden girl, little did she know, but she did not stand up for me, she admitted, alas love was defeated."

He falls asleep thinking of Desdemona, they were together in their separate dreams; she'd be in a short distance but he couldn't keep eye contact. The light bounced on her skin, and he'd catch a glimpse, he'd see the shape of her face and he'd be sure it was her. Then she'd vanish because he had limited time. His legs kicks like he's going to wake, he's losing the moment, but he'd see her soon or some day.

'Hallelujah for this chance to see your silhouette eye. Hallelujah for this life that I can't be there with you but I can dream. My apple tree; if your lip would save me let your kiss be my dying wish.'

The poet was her Invention, hers dangerously.

Chapter Three

Gold digging & Graveyard shifts.

{FLASHBACK; TWO YEARS BEFORE, May 7, 1957}

There would be tears said the poet, but the Duchess was a poetess with her body. In every position, she recited poetry. She was older and fragile, he did experiments with her body, they did freaky things in her lobby, the verandah, garden and her Mercedes. She was 75, 48 years older than Ólaf. She'd met him on Prize giving day, in the army locker room. The Medal of Honor was dedicated in her name "Duchess Adara's Golden Plate for Might and Valor". She was aged but looked very bright; one could tell she was a diva in her prime. She did not smile at all, her stare was blank, she had dull blue eyes and her white skin shrunk in the elbow. She wore pearls on both wrist and beryl around her neck. Her gown was turquoise blue, her hair looked like foam, she had clear white teeth and she was articulate in her speech. She stood firm and upright to the ground, she still had color, she had life in her, and she was dazzled by Ólaf's mannerism. She knew he could take care of her during her final days; she wanted him to be around. Ólaf was indulgent, he gave the sweet old lady the ride of her life, he dazzled her bones to tendon, she was flabbergasted by his chivalry, and he was a perfect gentleman. He knew how to touch the woman, and she sparkle for him, safe to say they met by coincidence as a matter of need.

Adara: Coincidence you say, sweet soldier.

Ólaf: Things do not just happen, if something happened; it is because a series of actions already occurred. That thing called coincidence can be an opportunity but if shrugged off, it's gone. Sometimes, that thing called coincidence is an eye opener or a warning sign; look away and fall victim. Sometimes, we are waiting for a coincidence.

Adara: hmm, and love is a whole different thing?

Olaf: My opinion of love is shaped by my experiences of life overtime. There's so many definitions and approach to love. Sometimes, it is all wrapped up in the love for a person, I believe in love and soul mates.

Adara: so when do these so called coincidences occur?

Ólaf: I think coincidences occur at a point where our mind is at and the things we have done… or the things people are doing for us. I think coincidence is as a result of our physical absence. For instance, I saw you in my dream because you thought of me last night, that's a coincidence. To be honest, there's not much I can do about my physical absence, I just hope for the best, and pray. Nothing would change because of a coincidence; a person would still handle situations with his or her good or bad character.

Adara: I used to believe in soul mates, now it looks delusional.

Ólaf: Well, soul mates are not meant for everyone, some people have different poisons. Some people don't love-

love as much as love wants to be loved. They don't get soul mates. Other people are all about love, all they can do is love, they may be broken and I hope they find their soul mate.

Adara: Do you think love to be steps well calculated before they're taken or some reckless actions of going all in? (She enquires).

Ólaf: Love is more than a profession, job or career. Love is an absolute feeling that overwhelms you at a point of no return. All you have to do is look forward. Love is the sea, love is the boat, and love is the sailor. Love is the wave and tide, love is the shark that consumes you when the boat capsizes. That moment you're in love, it's like being born again, love takes the wheel, but braces yourself just in case you're going to crash because love will survive and tell you not to give up. I know love is waiting for me and I'm looking forward to it.

Duchess Adara was the most beautiful young girl on Mary Boulevard in the 1880s. She got married to her first love at the age of 19, Lord Campbell II and he bore him no children. Lord Campbell II lost his life in an hostile takeover. She invented the Plate for Might and Valor to celebrate the Veterans and commemorate the lost soldiers. She too was a fierce woman, she knew what war cost. Ólaf had been warming her bed, he never made her feel alone, she was safe with him, and she was tighter than the girls on Unicorn Ln. She made more cream than the chocolate factory, and for the remainder of her life, he was her everything.

The moon illuminated the room from the left angle, as the curtain danced to the breeze from the balcony. The Duchess moaned softly, scratching on Ólaf's bare back, her slim pale fingers running down his spine leaving traces of her nails. His muscular body pounding harder on the older lady irrespective and she wanted more, he stared deep into her blank eyes for minutes, he did not blink, he thought of Desdemona, he wondered who was putting her in the family way. Adara stared straight into his tiny dark eyes squinting in the socket. She knew he had a lot on his mind or someone else had occupied his heart but she was going to experience the orgasmic blast. It was divine, divine… getting drunk off her Majesty; it rained cat and dog as they fucc. Rainy days like this gave him hibiscus memories. Ólaf rolled over the duchess then she lit a cigarette and sat on the left corner of the bed, she watched him pace around the room naked till he sat on the chair beside the windows such that Adara could see his reflection clearly in the mirror.

Adara: You think of her

Ólaf: All the time

Adara: Your thoughts bounce around the room, I can hear them clearly

Ólaf: Do not spite me for my weakness, its terror embedded in my soul. I don't know how to handle it anymore, I just sit and write in my textbook, the words I combine have no meaning, it can't be said but felt, it's sad she promised, but she left (He sobs).

Adara: I adore you for bravery and brevity but seeing you like this… vulnerable, tired and worn out, remind me that you're just a man, another decoration in the world, an expensive decoration. Now wipe your eyes fine man and chin up like the Wolf I fell for.

Ólaf picked up his textbook and wrote…

"It is intriguing, the bitter sweet story I tell. She fell in love with a gangster that's why I'm going to die there .I write in past tense when I reminisce everything she's said. My mind is on a rampage when I'm sleeping in another's bed. BDSM, because she wants pleasure and I deserve respect. The rain should wash the tears away, but I remember Thursday in the hill, June 15, 1950; it was cold so we made fire in embrace for warmth. We got talking about new stories like the old cinemas; with her bad body arched like a cat in the night, she initiated me with the juice in her private. I am her religion when she kneels down to pray. Together, we were wild animals, when I pulled up her short skirt and shifted her wet panties west, explosive orgasm, dog sex, thick sweat, bed wet, saying I love you from the deepest depth, till we were comfortable to give each other nicknames. I called her golden; she says I'm the best. In the days when our every hour was tough; I stayed ten toes down on the ground with my heart to the floor. Dear God, even if she may have forgotten me, don't let my love forsake me. I am stranded in her love cycle; her caterpillar has evolved into a butterfly. Her memories are curses; I'm stretched out on our love grave. I remember when I first met her,

our eyes overlapped, she'd just moved into the new house. Our first conversation was brief; it almost feels like she planted herself there intentionally, just for me to fall for her tricks."

Ólaf closed the book shut and gazed outside the windows to the open fields, and then he mumbled, *'how do you sleep without me beside you? You lied to every man that shared that bed with you.'*

On November 7, 1958, Duchess Adara died peacefully in her Palazzo. She had written off her properties to the possession of Ólaf. He was finally a wealthy man, not noble but wealthy. He had premonitions of Apostle putting a contract on his life so Ólaf retreated to one of the Duchess's cabin on an island in Ko Tao. It was breezy that evening and the trees were singing to the rhythm of the wind, the sky was pink and violet, meaning someone was crying to Eros, yelling cupid curse. Ólaf sat in the shower, the button-man could only hear water running and sniffling of the man in the bathroom. He had traced Ólaf all the way; he was waiting like a green snake in the grass as he canvassed the island for three months looking for the Cabin.

{FEBRUARY 16, 1959}

Ólaf slid into the tub, once again he forgot to shave like the previous day; he preferred to shave before his bath, he was hairy in the armpit and pelvic. He turned on hot water and whirlpool; he was exhausted, worn out, waiting for the perfect opportunity to have a dramatic reunion with Desdemona. He leaned backwards and dips deep in the bathtub as the Vinyl player shuffle melancholic music from the bedroom, he reminisces the day he first entered Apostle's Triangle.

{FLASHBACK 1st of April, 1947}

It was only a week after the Manifesto was published that Ólaf was introduced to Apostle as Roman J Esq.'s foster son. The white Limousine cruised into the mansion, and merry-go-round the water fountain in the drive way as Ólaf locked his on the Citadel. He thought, 'Rich kids do not have problems of need, they bother about attention and nail polish'. The Valet, a middle aged Caucasian man, looking exhausted in his black tailored tailcoat and top hat, walked briskly to take the door and usher Ólaf into the castle. The Valet spoke very fast, he hurried his words like he had rehearsed them the night before but still clear and articulate.

Valet: Bonsoir Monsieur, the young Lord and Lady are in the study, you need not come with manuals or textbooks next time, there are all the books of literature and history in the Library help yourself to it and make sure the children take an interest in you. (Assessing Ólaf -hair to loafer) Or you'd be fed to the crocodiles in the creek like the tutor before you. (Looks sternly at Ólaf who is shocked to hear the testimony, then he walks away) of course I am joking, now come, come.

Within the golden shade of the library, and the tall book shelves, a chandelier drops down in the center of the room from the high ceiling, illuminating the entire space moderately. Desdemona is spotted in a yellow shift dress, seated on a Chaise Longue, reading a small book with a red cover, title boldly written; *Tender is the night*. The ray of setting sun pierced through the soft curtains, kissing her skin, her tangerine body turned golden. Bishop, the younger son of Apostle stood in a corner by a Medieval armor suit, getting busy, strapping himself in war clothing, he was only 9 years old, but he knew what he wanted to be; a fighter for Arnold. They both seemed oblivious of Ólaf's presence.

Ólaf: (to Desdemona who would barely take a look at whoever he was) hello, my name is Ólafur; Ólaf for short, I'm the tutor. (The room is silent)

Ólaf: (he continues) um, what are you reading, my lady?

Desdemona: (sluggishly) Literature, Fitzgerald Literature

Ólaf: ah! Scott Fitzgerald's Jazz age

Desdemona: (smirk) Fine literature and top knowledge for who knows. (She slowly lifting her eyes to assess Olaf from his shoes) is that a loafer?

Ólaf: (calmly) Espadrille.

Desdemona: nice shoes.

Bishop: (struggling to carry himself in the heavy armor, walking like a zombie) I am Bishop, this is my sister Desdemona (swinging Hatori Hanzo blade) so what does 'mister fancy shoes' have for us?

Ólaf: short hand (smiles gently on one side of his cheeks)

Desdemona: Shorthand bores me to death. What about something dark and deep, with beautiful lyrics to serenade our sorrow.

Ólaf: Like an epitaph

Bishop: In shorthand?

Desdemona rolls her eyes, adjusting her Chiffon as she stretches her legs on the Chaise Longue, her shape like a Spanish guitar.

Desdemona: (plainly) no shorthand Bishop.

Bishop: (who had now gotten out of his armor finding a seat beside his sister, fondling her hair) Desdemona…

Desdemona: Yes, little brother?

Bishop: What is an epitaph?

Desdemona: An elegy (she grins, realizing she'd confused the little one even more).

Bishop frowns in ambiguity; he gets up and walks to the bookshelf. He grabs a stool for height to reach the top shelf, he picks a dictionary. Desdemona smiled as she watched her little brother flip the page of the dusty lexicon, her green eyes were enchanting, and they appeared innocent, so pure… She could get away with murder if she smiled at the jury.

Bishop gasps, 'an epitaph is a poem for the cemetery screen', he says.

Agatha barges into the library

Agatha: Bishop, Bish... (She mix eyes with Ólaf, almost shocked to see the stranger) and you are the tutor, I presume?

Ólaf: yes, I am Ólaf, My Lady

Agatha: And what are those shoes?

Desdemona: Espadrilles mother, they fit him.

Agatha : (sensing rudeness in her daughters tone, but fades it off with a fake smile then turns to Bishop) did you not hear me call, your Sensei is waiting in the Dojo.

Agatha holds Bishop by the hand and they walk out of the Library, she takes one last glance at Ólaf, she knew he was slightly impoverished, but he had a package to him.

Bishop: Mother, will Sensei teach Epitaph?

Agatha: No Bishop, martial art is similar to poetry in a unique way. (Their voices fade into the hallway).

Desdemona: Do you fancy painting?

Ólaf: Yes, I do, my lady.

Desdemona: Come, come, I'd show you something. (She slid her feet into a white fleece slippers and catwalks to the shelf, she pulls out a board from the behind and turned it over, it was a canvas— an unfinished painting of a woman holding a lamp, peeping at a man while he sleep.

Ólaf: (walking gently behind, his flat sole Espadrilles made no sound, he was astonished to learn the rich girl got her hands dirty with creativity) Eros and Psyche— Cupid's curse.

Desdemona: (her eyes glisten, her soul marvels at Olaf's intelligence quotient, indeed he is knowledgeable) wow, you know.

Ólaf: Writer and Painters are similar in a way; your canvas is like a diary.

Desdemona: The writer paints picture of memories with a pen; I am no writer, my words fail me. Although I have a textbook, I am still shy about my handwriting.

It's a beautiful confusion, how people from different roots could grow together in like minds. Like Desdemona, Psyche was cursed to love she would not see, and love itself was hurt. Psyche was a woman of extraordinary beauty, such beauty that angered the goddess of love of beauty, Aphrodite, who sent her son, Eros to punish the enchantress. Eros too is captivated by Psyche's beauty that he accidentally pricks himself with his own arrow, falling in love with her. He then visits her in secret, but she is not allowed to see his face. One night, influenced by curiosity, Psyche used a lamp to peep at Eros while he is asleep; struck by the sight of Eros (god of love), she accidentally burns him with the flame from her lamp and he wakes. Eros flees, never to meet Psyche again. Desdemona was obsessed with tragic fantasies, she was influenced by the habit, such that it reshaped her life and she was dramatic in every sense of it, and like Eros, Ólaf is bruised by cupid's arrow, cursed to fall in love with Desdemona.

***

The button-man took off his dessert boot and climbed up the stairs stealthily like a Ballerina. He opened the bedroom door gently, his revolver making an entrance before his body. His eyes ransacked the entire room in a flash to confirm if his prey was truly alone. On the wall with his bed beneath, Ólaf had a painting of Desdemona, and directly above on the ceiling too with sad orchestral blasting from the Gramophone on the shelf, the button-man read the name inscribed on the Vinyl with a sharp glance, "beating memories", then he took another look at the painting on the wall, he dropped his revolver and head with empathy and immediately he realized he had to keep it professional. He continued tracing the sniffling sound coming from the bathroom, the running water had left steam in the air, the sniffling stopped, only water running, the button-man walked in; the steam making it difficult to see, Ólaf appeared behind him, naked, grabbing him and locking his neck in his left arm, his right hand contesting for the loaded revolver. The button-man jabbed Ólaf with his elbow then Ólaf bit his right ear, the button-man screamed; the revolver fell from his hand and slid to the water closet. Ólaf applied pressure, his teeth's all bloody, Ólaf bit off his ear then kicked him in the arse as he groan in pain. The button-man cried like a little child and crawled on, holding on to dear life. Ólaf picked up the revolver and squeezed the trigger; the bullet exploded in his forehead, in the centre of his eyes, the button-man *shit* himself.

Ólaf frisked the dead button-man to find some information; he picked the cell phone in his Jacket and dialed the last incoming call, the receiver picked before the phone got a chance to ring once.

Apostle: Is it done?

Ólaf kept mute and hung, Apostle wanted him gone. He searched the pocket of the dead button-man's pleated pants and removed his wallet, his mouth was still bloody. He found a card with an address written on it then he washed himself in the shower, picked a few clothes and hurried out before torching the Cabin.

Chapter Four

Apostle's Triangle

{IN THE GIANT COURTROOM, SILENCE OVERWHELMS)

Chevalier reads from Ólaf's big book…

'Wealthy and alone, bitter feelings deterrent to my soul. There's a sudden calm in the pain from loneliness, it'd only make it easier if you were at peace with yourself. Sometimes, it is okay to showcase the skeletons in your shelf. If his blood brother would choose sides, he'd go with the opponent, I fear my closest friend. There'd been a division in their little organization, and he was standing alone. He knew better than to kill a butterfly; if you've been imprisoned before, you'd know a bird exists to fly. He set the dreams aside, the other was overprotective, I guess he was holding on to something else, his own dream, after all, they are separate beings. - The beauty of their friendship; they once shared the same dream. Independence is a curse to my kind, sadly I cherish friendship in mankind. There was a black hole on his back, beneath his left shoulder, on the back wall of his heart. He'd been stabbed too many times, with several objects; dagger, spear, kitchen knife - by the ones who he broke bread with, either they forgot him too quickly and easily, or they counted him out intentionally. Maybe his ideas pissed them off or he did not have the best behavior, but his sweat and blood had watered their

friendship for so many years, he wouldn't have predicted the betrayal sooner or ever. -But these things did happen.

Always, he was alone on his mental, wishing he had someone to talk to, but betrayal resonated louder, confining him to his lonely, and suddenly… it all happened suddenly. He was a bitter person too, he would be a better person if he could, but he had no one to talk to. Their little organization had changed the tone of their friendship; they were more concerned about channeling their dreams towards making the money. Their definitions of life changed along the way; a woman came in their way. It was a sad story to tell everyday because love can never be judged. Anything done in the name of love is foolishness. He was a fool for her, but it was the normal thing.

Sadness overwhelms my heart when I'm alone, I think about things, again and again. It is a shame. I blame my self for everything, I am to blame. Maybe I am a terrible person, the assuming begins; I should have done things differently. What use is all the money when you're alone every season, valentine, Eid al fitr and New Year's Eve? If nobody wants you, you're a terrible person. Or you don't want anybody but one person.

It is beautiful how words of poetry can solve problems pertaining to the soul, it is the only therapy for the returning soldiers, it may not fix the broken bones, but the pain could cease for a minute, I am in need of that relief, poetic justice. We are all human beings and we possess special gifts, it is only the ignorant whose points aren't valid but we'd remain attentive, a wise man said nothing and the foolish brought ideas to him. This is only a summary of the war in a nutshell, but love conquered all, love is the atomic weapon, the explosive energy and the disastrous molecules that broke down the temple, rebuilding it in three days, leaving wonders for all. Love yours desirously.'

Duchess in the audience: How broken can the writer be?

Chevalier, the Rat: (Laughter engulfs his soul… these were the right questions, someone was paying attention).

-The writer is hurt from time to time, questions of… what could have been?

-The writer is a perfectionist, but terrible with punctuation, the writer is just another human being; imperfect and incomplete, bloody degenerate with addictions and excesses, or maybe he's ancestrally driven and he always had it in him, maybe he was young when they started to live in him and he was pulling strings, maybe he was young when they started manifesting in his doings. Now he can't stop doing it. - Questions of… what could have been?

Silence engulfs the court room as they processed the allegations tendered by Chevalier against Apostle.

Chevalier, the Rat: Apostle is corrupt; he acquired wealth from manipulating others. I was there, I was in the room that faithful day, I have it all recorded in the tapes. Every evil man would fall; Apostle knew his time would come.

Lady: Liar!!!

Lord Velvet: Impossible!!!

Courtroom deputy: Order!!!

Chevalier, the Rat: One blue evening, I received a letter in my mailbox with an address inside a textbook, this book, my friend needed a favor. He asked me to bear witness to a face off. (Wipes his eyes with his tie) you see, to understand my friend, I had to take you through his humble beginning. Ólaf was not really my friend, but he noticed me, I was always in his pictures on the battlefield. So when I received his letter, I knew the time had come to put my loyalty to test. (He fills his cup with water and took a gulp) Loyalty, I speak of loyalty like the breath I breathe, you don't come by loyalty easily, only a few spirit resonate with me. Loyalty is a thread, put inside a needle in a dark place and very accurate. Loyalty is assuring, loyalty is a pat in the back in silence, loyalty is a reoccurring occurrence, loyalty can't be bought with gold or foreign currency, loyalty is embedded in true friendship. (He heaved a great sigh of despair), every soldier has been bought with money. Loyalty is faded, there is no more loyalty, it would come like visitor but you can't see it, yet you get the picture. You see, to get into the Triangle, I had to fabricate a lie…
Chevalier flips the pages of the book and continues to read:

{FLASHBACK, 19 JANUARY, 1960}

I speak for her, and I'm accurate; she's my soul mate. My girl, my bouncing flowery golden girl. You will love me by fire and force, You will love my hair and my voice, you will love the feel of my touch, you will love me in the Mosque or Church, you will love my pride and my scent, you will love my guilt and innocence, you will love the prints of my steps, you will have no choice, because I got you by fire and force.

Desdemona: Mama I am never going to marry Prince Charming, Sej, he makes me nauseous. He lies, he speaks like the serpent, he pretends. Mama I have met a man like none other, they wouldn't let me speak his name.

Desdemona kneels by the corner of her bed; she's talking to the Holy Mother.

Desdemona: Mama, let me speak his name, it's more than a decade he's been away, no more letters, I should have replied those mails, Mama I feel my heart tear to pieces, can he come to me?

Agatha stomps into the room; she's astonished to see her daughter in a wretched way.

Agatha: It's been raining all day, Desdemona, get your sweater or you'd catch the flu.

Desdemona: (stuck in daydream) he would fit me, he would fit me better than my favorite sweater. Mama I met a man, but he's not noble. Mama I fell in love with him within a split second. Mama my heart is racing, I will run to him.

Agatha: Desdemona, pull yourself together; you are no longer a child. Your father wants you to marry from the higher ranks.

Desdemona retreats to her closet and slid into a black backless gown, she puts on black lip stick and ferronnières on her head. Agatha spots Desdemona's gold cover textbook on the dresser, she flips the pages and there it was; Desdemona's testimonial to Olaf's undying relentless affection. Agatha gets upset and waltz off with the book; at the parlor on the ground floor, Agatha throws Desdemona's textbook into the fireplace. Every word, letters in ink on the pages of the textbook dissolves into flame. Agatha's is outraged; she hisses and walks out into the hallway.

****

Noblemen wine and dine; it is no news that the governments have been corrupt from time. Apostle was seen as an honest figure; denizens believe he got his name from his deeds and not at birth. Apostle, now 2IC in the royal military, second in command in charge of social responsibility and public relation of ARNOLD's administration. Apostle was first exalted when he architect the master plan for the Great Arnold who defeated the Nersus in the first brutal siege, making popular the phrase 'ARNOLD, the Subjugator'. Agatha, wife of Apostle, mother of Desdemona and Bishop; she looked much older than Apostle, one would wonder how a man like Apostle would wound up with a woman such as Agatha. Everyone say he married her for her prowess.

Her father was Lord, right hand to the first Emperor before Arnold. Agatha on the hand would always keep neat, walking in her silk robe and high heels at 2 in the morning. She sleeps like a diva, just so Apostle would not get tired of her.

There's a loud cheer at the reception, Bishop and the army generals walk into the room.

Desdemona: (running into Bishop's embrace) oh dear brother, come, come, let me clean you up dear brother.

Bishop: (big grin across his handsome young face) my sister, my first love, with a single strike of my sword, I'd smite any man who dears to look at you in a way I do not approve of. You were on my mind all through the war.

APOSTLE: My boy, Bishop the careful. You have made me proud. (Apostle kisses Bishop on both cheeks and embraces him). We will enjoy this life forever, let us toast. – Now with whiskey in our vein, (his eyes ransacked the room then he winks at Agatha) we are the lucky ones, let us spread out and lay our branches to the sun… And when the moon is upon us, remember we are subjugators.

The door slams open for Prince Charming, Sej, bearing letters from the province. Sej, Sejius, son of Narcissus- half brother of ARNOLD. Dirty men make the loudest noise, he never took a defeat in the war or in an argument, he was hard as a rock, heady to a fault, and very full of himself, he had a square shaped head and his hair was blonde, he had his haircut like in the military force. His eyes were brown and he had a strong stare, he looked like someone who could revolt if he was not paid attention to.

Sej: you look well Desdemona (takes her by her hand and kiss the back of her palm) pardon my eccentricity, Apostle you look dapper.

Valet: (walks briskly into the room, interrupting the conversation) Pardon me sire, but the guest should wait in the Throne room. (A stern look on his face).

Sej: Ahh yes!

Valet: Come with me sire. (Escorts Sej to the throne room)

Four men, three unworthy men, able bodied men, extremely wealthy men, are gathered in Apostle's Triangle, to ask the hand of his enchantress daughter, Desdemona in marriage, with Ólaf present. He wore a brown Tweed suit with burgundy design cravat underneath his white shirt and a brown penny loafer on his feet that complemented his pants with a unique style. As he gazed and explored the throne room, his eye caught the painting of 'a starry night', the works of Van Gogh and he thought, *'golden man, golden mind, que sera sera, chance and opportunity with peace of mind'*. He looked at himself through the shiny chalice in his hands and said *'I am golden'*. An overwhelming sadness had taken away his appetite and he did not know why, the orchestras made him cry. He was back in the house where love taught him, now the love had come back to taunt him. He said,' *indeed we are wanting attention from whoever cares gives it to us the most. Me too, I'm trying my best, I don't want to fucc up'.*

Eventually, Ólaf was back for his golden girl. He could win her heart all over again if he was asked to give a speech, he already prepared a note for it, but the other men would result to bragging; The Monte Carlo, The Hacienda, the mob boss, the blackmailer with a loaded revolver, none of whom made honest money; stock exchange, bonds, security, fashion industry, they had nothing to keep the conversation going on how excess demand affect supply in the capital market. Then the know-it-all, Prince Charming Sej, who spoke awfully loud and a lot, he dwells on the attention.

Chevalier, the rat, he thinks he is the smartest one, and although we tend to judge people by their evil, we never know what they too have been through, he had a scar on his face, to his left eye, like a long slice from a dagger. He would sit stiff like a statue for minutes, if you took some time to observe, you'd think your world had paused, just then his eyes would ravage the room like a hurricane, to capture every scene like a Kodak movie lens. The muscles of his ear would stretch and thicken like a rabbit each time a new voice echoed, he was a cassette tape, with the eyes of an owl, and like an owl he looked scary. He was short, dark, chubby and stiff, even his sentences were brief and full of profanity. He wore a white shirt and Castleton green corduroy under a russet chesterfield and brown leather brogues on his feet.

Esteban looked wicked and dangerous; he did not even need to speak. He was in his early 30s. Lanky Caucasoid, and never looked anyone in the eyes, men like that are terrible to trust. He wore a fake smile always, probably how he managed to get those politicians and monarchs under his arm. He had a tiny voice when he managed to speak, a voice that did not fit his person but his Burgundy double breasted suit would make you take a second look.

Sej: I was Captain of the 4th battalion, Nursing Bottle, Pink Sky and Red Sea. Twenty soldiers were trained to launch a specific military weapon of mass destruction. Nine men went rogue, killing the rest and stealing the weapon, I was summoned by ARNOLD, sent out by the highest hierarchy to return order. I don't bargain with terrorists, I murder. After the war my scars were covered by all the glamour and splendor, some things the foot soldiers do not stand to benefit. More often than not, money is the base of riot, so I stand to gain in the war by trading ammunitions, they cost more.

Esteban: Do you close your eyes to sleep in the night?

Sej: I have recurring dreams, the priest calls it nightmare, and I take barbital in excess. My prowess cover my darkness, I keep my skeletons in my top shelve, but a soldier must survive, after all I too have protected a million lives.

Esteban: We all have skeletons Prince Charming, but I don't keep mine in my shelf, I bury them outside in my yard, my dogs do the digging. Money you say is the base of war. Yes, and money makes the richest more corrupt. I have forged signatures of dignitaries and blackmail the monarchs who jumped into business to cover their looted treasury. Behind closed door, they crawled on their knees to my feet, reminding me of the times when they fed me in their dining. I look to them with so much disgust; they called me a simple man, now I have their balls in my palm.

Chevalier, the Rat: I read the book of Machiavelli, I have read the Mafia Manager by V, and I was consigliere to the great Capo Corleone in Sicily. I have come a long way beyond the Equestrian Fields to Apostles Triangle because I am determined.

Esteban: Yet, you're called the Rat.

Chevalier, the Rat: (abruptly) Rat because I couldn't go down for what I did not participate in, the great Capo was out of control, I thought of my Wife and kids who weren't grown.

Sej: (Sharply) but you did some killing too

Chevalier, the Rat: I did not! I gave orders to kill for the great Capo. (He drops his head with regret) and once I killed myself in protection custody, I overdosed on sleeping pills.

Esteban: We all have our sad life.

Silence envelope the room like dark curtains, for a moment they had forgotten the reason they were in

Apostle's Triangle. They were brutal men, they were changed men and they were still changing.

Ólaf was reading his big story where he sat. The room was big enough for five hundred guests; it had eleven large windows with extra sized curtains opened wide, making the room airy.

Esteban: (Intruding) …and who are you? You could be a serial killer; these other men are no better. (With a whiskey glass in hand, pointing to Ólaf) What do you have in your big book?

Ólaf: I am writing a beautiful script, but every now and then inspiration dries up like golden leaves. It is a different feeling when you rule your world; you make the decisions and no bargaining or negotiation. You just do it. When you're wealthy you do it, mind you, wealth is embedded in the frame of mind. Not everyone is fit to be wealthy, some people are just rich and some they bully. The only thing wealth and riches have in common is money, wealth is timid, rich is shiny. Money means opportunity, money miss road, some people are scared of money, some people learn the hard way, some people work harder, some are smarter, some of them are the brave ones, some of them are very religious, and very because; I don't know any more.

Esteban: (he frowns hard at Ólaf, understanding the depth of his parable, words he had combine from liquor, he was bruised deeply in his feelings because he understood… he understood the beautiful chaos in fine poetry) you are the saddest of us all, permit me not to speak with you anymore.

A gentleman's words are in a gentleman's quote, the elite wine and dine with a code. For Ólaf, after the war, nothing seemed all that amazing. Not till that moment when their paths crossed and their eyes collude in the hall, two eyes turned four. The Valet who had been standing silent in a corner of Throne room exclaims:

Valet: All hail the Noble Ecclesiastes!

Chapter Five

Thugs of War

Rushing into the Throne Room ahead of Apostle and Bishop, Agatha chasing behind, Desdemona runs into the arms of her lover, Olaf. They had not seen one another for over a decade. Oh Desdemona, fine woman, tall and slender, with perky breasts, oval face like a perfect egg, and her eyes were still green. Her teeth's were no longer milky and she used braces as a kid, now just aesthetics. She stands upright and you can carve out her curves, her breast and buttocks, they are perfect like brackets. Her gown overflow, she wears peach in the summer, and in the fall she wears troubled orange. Her hair is light brown and long, not like Rapunzel, but you get the idea. Her heroic overture made her look manly but it came with another shade of beauty, she is magnetic, she is majestic, she only speaks to few people, she is credulous, and her aura is visible golden. The gentle steps of her heel while she's cat walking, the perfecto of her hips, God is an artist. Her feet are slender like her body, her toes descend chronologically and the clearness of her nails, like a goddess, a man like me would fall to my knees and kiss her feet because it is my fetish.

Ólaf: That's my girl, my meadow moon, human crystal, Rose petals; her memories put the smile on my face during the war, son of nobody. She illuminates the room, every man's head turn, the bravado in her allure, she defeats everybody; the Army general, the movers, the blackmailers and the shakers, the poet and the writer. Expensive girl, candy necklace, Lana Del Rey, River enchantress, just like a goddess she chose me.

Apostle: You miserable, I have tried everything to get rid of you. You're hemorrhoid to my skin!

Ólaf: You can only lock Desdemona in your castle or boarding school, but her love would always roam free with me.

(How she looked him in the eye, she would never look another the way she looked at him. Ólaf grabs Desdemona closer; she holds him tighter as she trembles and tear).

Apostle: (eyes colored red with rage) take your hands off my Daughter this instance or you'd receive the tails end of my sword. (Draws out Hatori Hanzo blade).

Desdemona: Papa, kill this man and you have killed me too, I shall not forgive you (she cries).

Apostle: Desdemona my apple, you don't know what fits you (he cries out)

Desdemona: papa, he fits me better than your favorite suit.

Agatha: (runs across the room, kneels and beckons on Sej) do something young man, aren't you Prince Charming anymore, you say you love my daughter and you watch her world crumble before your eyes, you are a coward. Do something!

Sej: (snapping out of his confusion to take authority, facing Ólaf) Bollock! You can't fool us with your fancy words. What's your last name, you are nobody! To think you can razzle dazzle us with sweet words.

Ólaf: my father was Dmitri, the brave goldsmith and my tutors; Roman J Esq. and Ingrid, my mother. I may not be born polished, but I shine brighter than the stars in the moonlight.

Chevalier, the Rat: (laughing out loud) I like this one. You managed to survive by looking harmless I suppose.

Ólaf: No, I fought like every brave men on Cornflower fields. I am a survivor, not everyone survived the war.

Esteban: (reaching in his coat for his revolver) this writer has managed to set a new tone for our gracious gathering. (Points the gun at Ólaf) your presence is a plague!

Everyone's taken aback.

Valet: You sneaked a revolver into the Throne Room you filthy man.

Esteban: (with an evil grin on his face) you think I would trust rich men without self assurance? You think I am stupid like the others? I am never going to take uncalculated risks. Never!

Sej: (Taking few steps away from Esteban and Ólaf). I should have known better than to bring a knife to a gun fight.

Ólaf: I came with nothing but a pen and this book.

Chevalier, the Rat: and how do you presume you'd win this battle. I am strapped up with a recording tape for you all's blackmail (laughing sarcastically).

Ólaf: Love, love conquers all I presume.

Sej : (draws out his knife furiously at Ólaf) how dear you make mockery of power you wretch. Gold digger, you carry wealth that doesn't belong to you, you became a celebrity off the opportunities of the battle field. Then you waltz in here and talk about love as a weapon. You should die this instance.

She knew him like the back of her palm, and he looked like Art, he was shaped like a man carved by the hands of Michelangelo, he was well built to the abs, and perfect like Michelangelo breathe life into him. He was scrumptious to look at. His presence carried the air of relief, like she loved to be around him, he knew how to talk to everybody, he was polished, polite and poise, his words were smooth, too sweet, his mouth was like a beehive, and his saliva was honey.

Ólaf: (his eyes piercing into Agatha's eyes with pity, he knew Apostle needed no further convincing, then he turns to look at Desdemona) I wrote you those poems under the pink sky when I told God; it is you that would fit me better than my favorite sweater. It was catastrophic, I would lay on the bed with the Duchess, desperately thinking how you should be by my side, and if you'd write me, I'd be quick to reply. You never replied

Desdemona: (Her beautiful green eyes filled with shame, pity and regret) I kept a notebook

Agatha: I burned your notebook

Desdemona: Mother!!!! (She cried)

Chevalier the Rat: Women? I surrender. Fight over a woman, I shall not. I shall not betroth a woman who has her heart out for another. She could slither me in bed. I fear these women.

Agatha: (Spits on the ground at Olaf) you're not noble, you're just a gold digger, I shall bear no special room in my heart for your love of my daughter, so get out. You don't belong here.

Esteban: (furious) Oh! What is this madness? How would a con man get into the Triangle in the first place?

Chevalier, the Rat: the Triangle was built by the earliest scammers, I am not surprised.

Sej: (interrupts) keep quiet this minute snitch. I would smite you to death in a blow. What happens in the triangle stays in the triangle.

Bishop: For once, let us all not act barbarically. We are all exhausted from the trauma on Cornflower field. Why don't we sit and settle this amicably, or duel if we must. Whoever is fit to come first, wins.

Sej: (knowing well he may lose to Ólaf, after all, his victories were Bishop's in the first place) this disgust is not fit for my blade, he should take his own life this instance! (Holding his knife firmer, stretching it at Olaf, a sweat drop from his head, he wipes it off with the back of his left palm).

Ólaf: (grabs Desdemona tighter, looking into her eyes with a tender smile on one cheek) the best love song I wrote in the coldest winter, I want your body on a platter. I have written a lot of books, beautiful poetry attributes to my name. Millions of words have been combined by yours sincerely, you were my muse, but I do not have the perfect words to replace I love you, so I have to make you feel special, to make myself feel special. The pride of a man is his woman; you look like me and that is enough.

Desdemona: Baby we need to leave, I'm getting drunk on your noble deeds. You are the only noble spirit I know, so let's go.

They both hold hands and run across the throne room to the exit door, Sej charged towards Ólaf and separates their bond, Desdemona falls on the floor, Agatha wails.

Agatha: My Precious!

Sej: (punching Ólaf in the face) you would not take what belongs to another, gold digger! You would never get away with this one.

Bishop: (jumps in to separate both men) take the brawl to the arena; don't spill blood on this expensive tapestry!

Ólaf kicks Sej away from him as Desdemona struggles to get up in the arms of Agatha.

Apostle: Look at the menace you caused in my house, you mad man! Orphaned mad man! I told Roman J Esq. to do away with you; he said you were too precious! Now look what you caused, I had to take out a great man for your existence. The letter bomb was my invention, you're a plague indeed! (Apostle kicks Ólaf in the chest, as he falls and tries to get up, Apostle continues kicking).

Desdemona: Mother, leave me! Papa, don't kill him. I love him, I hate you people!

Apostle: Desdemona, my apple! You'd love me later. (Throws another kick at Ólaf but he misses).

Sej: Shoot this man Esteban, it'd be an honor.

Desdemona breaks free from her Mother's grip and run to her lover's arm. Esteban fired a kill shot, the bullet pierced into Desdemona's heart and Ólaf's simultaneously.

Agatha: (screams) No! (She slumps).

Apostle: (cries out to Esteban) what have you done? You imbecile!

Bishop immediately grabs the revolver and launched a bullet into Esteban's skull, Esteban dies instantly. Chevalier, who had been taken aback by terror- *'who would have thought the recorder inside his coat would be the big story'*, he thought, while Prince Charming Sej fled the scene.

Ólaf: (Desdemona breathes faintly in his arms) hush, don't speak my darling; don't speak (coughing and spiting blood).

Desdemona: Sometimes words get trapped in my mind, sometimes I don't know how to handle how I feel. Other times I spend doubting everything I know, but there's no doubt about this, I figured it out, I love you (she gasps for her last breath and dies in his arm).

Ólaf: (tears rolling down his eyes) I could have sworn that you'd be the one for me. I don't know what I did, but I'm still paying for my sin. If I knew you'd fly away, I'd have cut down your wings and put you in a cage, I'd have locked you in my heart forever, just so you would stay. A time in a man's life when love is the essence. (He gasps for his last breath and dies in her grasp).

Arnold: a tragic story you tell, now sadness overwhelms the audience, but what good is a story if it doesn't make you shed tears.

Courtroom deputy: It is a wrap Monsieur Chevalier; Apostle took his life; Bullet and Knife. Lady Agatha is locked up in the asylum, Bishop has returned to war… and Esteban, the common thug on the street, recruited by powerful men for use in politics, erased. Your textbook and record tape will end up in the evidence locker, and if luck would shine on it, it may be put to use as a movie script or documentary on the big screen. However, it is difficult to believe the Noble Apostle would be tangled up with a miscreant such as you, therefore you must refrain from saying him name ever again. Your amnesty report should state clearly that you were pardoned for your activism in the war on Cornflower fields, but you must leave Mary Boulevard forever. This Alpha City will not continue to accommodate men of your sort, even though you should be silenced at once. So take a bow and take your leave.

The audience cheered with standing ovation and resounding applause, exalting the judgment meted out on Chevalier by the great Arnold, the subjugator. The people were dogmatic and sheepish in their follower-ship. Chevalier took a bow and a last look at the audience; he was disappointed, if only they had met the man in the story, or the golden girl, his muse. His head dropped in disappointment as he walked out of the courtroom, the audience begin to boo.

BALLAD OF A GOLDEN GIRL

Printed in Great Britain
by Amazon

44724068R00050